Licensed exclusively to Top That Publishing Ltd
Tide Mill Way, Woodbridge, Suffolk, IP12 1AP, UK
www.topthatpublishing.com

0 2 4 6 8 9 7 5 3 1
Manufactured in China

Written by Joshua George
Illustrated by Sarah Lawrence

ISBN 978-1-78700-277-7

A catalogue record for this book is available from the British Library

For Dad, thanks for all the bedtime stories

ROAR! went the lion

by **Joshua George**
& **Sarah Lawrence**

'Roar!' went the lion ...

'Baa!' **went the cow ...**

'Moo!' went the wolf ...

'Oink!' went the owl ...

'Twit-twoo!'

went the pig ...

'Cluck!' went the frog ...

'Awoooo!'
went the sheep ...

'Bzzzz!' went the dog ...

'Ribbit!' went the bee ...

'Woof!'

went the hen ...

'Stop, stop!

You've got it all wrong, let's start again!'

'Roar!'
went the lion ...
'Moo!' went the cow ...

'Awoooo!'

went the wolf ...

'Twit twoo!'
went the owl ...

'Oink!'

went the pig ...

'Ribbit!'
went the frog ...

'Baa!'
went the sheep ...

'Woof!' went the dog ...

'Bzzz!'
went the bee ...

'Cluck!'
went the hen ...

'Goodness me, what was all that noise? Now please be quiet and go to sleep!'

'Roar!'
went the lion ...

'Yay, let's start again!'